The
Fairy Doll

Also by Rumer Godden
and published by Macmillan Children's Books

The Diddakoi
The Story of Holly and Ivy
The Dolls' House
Miss Happiness and Miss Flower

For older readers

The Peacock Spring
The Greengage Summer

RUMER GODDEN

The Fairy Doll

Illustrated by Gary Blythe

MACMILLAN CHILDREN'S BOOKS

First published 1956 by Macmillan

This edition published 2006 by Macmillan Children's Books
a division of Macmillan Publishers Limited
20 New Wharf Road, London N1 9RR
Basingstoke and Oxford
www.panmacmillan.com

Associated companies throughout the world

ISBN-13: 978-0-330-44226-8
ISBN-10: 0-330-44226-0

1 3 5 7 9 8 6 4 2

A CIP catalogue record for this book is available from
the British Library.

Typeset by Intype Libra Ltd
Printed and bound in Great Britain by Mackays of Chatham plc, Kent

For Rose Mary because, once upon a time,
I am afraid we treated her as Christabel, Godfrey and
Josie treated Elizabeth before she had the fairy doll.

Chapter 1

Nobody knew where she came from.

'She must have belonged to Mother when Mother was a little girl,' said Father, but Mother did not remember it.

'She must have come from Father's house, with the Christmas decorations,' said Mother, but Father did not remember it.

As long as the children could remember, at Christmas every year, the fairy doll had been there at the top of the Christmas tree.

She was six inches high and dressed in a white gauze dress with beads that sparkled; she had silver wings, and a narrow silver crown on her dark hair, with a glass dewdrop in front that sparkled too; in one of her hands she had a silver wand, and on her

feet were silver shoes – not painted, stitched. 'Fairies must have sewn those,' said Mother.

'Or mice,' said Christabel, who was the eldest.

Elizabeth, the youngest, was examining the stitches.

'Fairy mice,' said Elizabeth.

You may think it is a lucky thing to be the youngest, but for Elizabeth it was not lucky at all; she was told what to do – or what not to do – by her sisters and brother all day long, and she was always being left out or made to stay behind.

'You can't come, you're too young,' said Christabel.

'You can't reach. You're too small,' said Godfrey, who was the only boy.

'You can't play. You're too little,' said Josie. Josie was only two years older than Elizabeth, but she ordered her about most of all.

Christabel was eight, Godfrey was seven, Josie was six, but Elizabeth was only four and she was different from the others: they were thin, she was fat; their legs were long, hers were short; their hair was curly, hers was straight; their eyes were blue, hers were grey and easily filled with tears. They rode bicycles; Christabel's was green, Godfrey's was red, Josie's dark blue. Elizabeth rode the old tricycle; the paint had come off, and its wheels went 'Wh-ee-ze, wh-ee-ze, wh-ee-ze.'

'Slowpoke,' said Christabel, whizzing past.

'Tortoise,' said Godfrey.

'Baby,' said Josie.

'Not a slowpoke, tortoise, baby,' said Elizabeth but they did not hear; they were far away, spinning down the hill. 'Wh-ee-ze, wh-ee-ze, wh-ee-ze,' went the tricycle, and Elizabeth's eyes filled with tears.

'Cry-baby,' said Josie, who had come pedalling back, and the tears spilled over. Then that Christmas, Elizabeth saw the fairy doll.

She had seen her before, of course, but, 'Not really,' said Elizabeth; not properly, as you shall hear.

Every year there were wonderful things on the Christmas tree: tinsel and icicles of frosted glass that had been Father's when he was a little boy; witch balls in colours like jewels and a trumpet of golden glass – it had been Father's as well – and bells that were glass too but coloured silver and red. Have you ever rung a glass bell? Its clapper gives out a 'ting' that is like the clearest, smallest, sweetest voice.

There were silvered nuts and little net stockings filled with gold and silver coins. Can you guess what the coins were? They were chocolate. There were transparent boxes of rose petals and violets and mimosa. Can you guess what *they* were? They were sweets.

There were Christmas crackers and coloured lights and candles.

When the lights were lit, they shone in the dewdrop on the fairy doll's crown, making a bead of light; it twinkled when anybody walked across the room or touched the tree, and the wand stirred in the fairy doll's hand. 'She's alive!' said Elizabeth.

'Don't be silly,' said Christabel, and she said scornfully, '*What* a little silly you are!'

Thwack. A hard small box of sweets fell off the tree and hit Christabel on the head.

The fairy doll looked straight in front of her, but the wand stirred gently, very gently, in her hand.

In the children's house, on the landing, was a big chest carved of cedar wood; blankets were stored in it, and spare clothes. The Christmas things were kept there too; the candles had burned down, of

course, and the crackers had been snapped and the
sweets and nuts eaten up, but after Christmas
everything else was packed away; last of all the
fairy doll was wrapped in blue tissue paper, put in
a cotton-reel box, laid with the rest in the cedar
chest, and the lid was shut.

When it was shut, the chest was still useful.
Mother sent the children to sit on it when they were
naughty.

*

The next Christmas Elizabeth was five. 'You can help to dress the tree,' said Mother and gave her some crackers to tie on. 'Put them on the bottom branches, and then people can pull them,' said Mother.

The crackers were doll-size, silver, with silver fringes; they were so pretty that Elizabeth did not want them pulled; she could not bear to think of them tattered and torn, and she hid them in the moss at the bottom of the tree.

'*What* are you doing?' said Godfrey in a terrible voice.

He had been kneeling on the floor with his stamp collection, for which he had a new valuable purple British Guiana stamp. He jumped up and jerked the crackers out.

'You're afraid of the bang so you hid them,' he said.

Elizabeth began to stammer 'I – I wasn't – ' But he was already jumping round her, singing, 'Cowardy, cowardy custard.'

'Cowardy, cowardy custard . . .'

A gust of wind came under the door, it lifted up the new valuable purple British Guiana stamp and blew it into the fire.

The fairy doll looked straight in front of her, but the wand stirred gently, very gently, in her hand.

Elizabeth was often naughty; she did not seem able to help it, and that year she spent a great deal of time sitting on the cedar chest.

As she sat, she would think down through the cedar wood, and the cotton-reel box, and the blue tissue paper, to the fairy doll inside.

Then she did not feel quite as miserable.

*

The Christmas after that she was six; she was allowed to tie the witch balls and the icicles on the tree but not to touch the trumpet or the bells. 'But I can help to light the candles, can't I?' asked Elizabeth.

Josie had been blowing up a balloon; it was a green balloon she had bought with her own money, and she had blown it to a bubble of emerald. You must have blown up balloons, so that you will know what hard work it is. Now Josie took her lips away for a moment and held the balloon carefully with her finger and thumb.

'Light the candles!' she said to Elizabeth. 'You? You're far too young.'

Bang went the balloon.

The fairy doll looked straight in front of her, but the wand stirred gently, very gently, in her hand.

Under the tree was a small pale blue bicycle, shining with paint and steel; it had a label that read: ELIZABETH.

'You lucky girl,' said Mother.

The old tricycle was given to a children's home; it would never go 'wh-ee-ze, wh-ee-ze' for Elizabeth again. She took the new bicycle and wheeled it carefully onto the road. 'You lucky girl,' said everyone who passed.

Elizabeth rang the bell and once or twice she put her foot on the pedal and took it off again. Then she wheeled the bicycle home.

That year Elizabeth was naughtier than ever and seemed able to help it less and less.

She spilled milk on the Sunday newspapers before Father had read them; she broke Mother's Wedgwood bowl, and by mistake she mixed the paints in Christabel's new paint box. 'Careless little idiot,' said Christabel. 'I told you not to touch.'

When Mother sent Elizabeth to the shop she forgot matches or flour or marmalade, and Godfrey had to go and get them. 'You're a perfect duffer,' said Godfrey, furious. Going to dancing, she dropped the penny for her bus fare, and Josie had to get off the bus with her.

'I'll never forgive you. Never,' said Josie.

It grew worse and worse. Every morning when they were setting off to school, 'Elizabeth, you haven't brushed your teeth,' Christabel would say, and they had to wait while Elizabeth went back. Then they scolded her all the way to school.

At school it was no better. She seemed more silly and stupid every day. She could not say her tables, especially the seven-times; she could not keep up in reading, and when she sewed, the cloth was all over bloodspots from the pricks. The other children laughed at her.

'Oh Elizabeth, why are you such a stupid c₁
asked Miss Thrupp, the teacher.

Sometimes, that year, Elizabeth got down
behind the cedar chest, though it
was dusty there, and lay
on the floor. 'I wish
it was Christmas,'
she said to
the fairy doll
inside. Then
she would remember
something else and say, 'I wish
it never had been Christmas,' because worst of all,
Elizabeth could not learn to ride her bicycle.

Father taught her, and Mother taught her;
Christabel never stopped teaching her. 'Push,
pedal; pedal pedal pedal,' cried Christabel, but
Elizabeth's legs were too short.

'Watch me,' said Godfrey, 'and you won't
wobble.' But Elizabeth wobbled.

'Go fast,' said Josie. 'Then you won't fall.' But
Elizabeth fell.

All January, February, March, April, and June
she tried to ride the bicycle. In July and August they

went to the sea so that she had a little rest; in September, October, November she tried again, but when December came, I am sorry to tell you, Elizabeth still could not ride the bicycle.

'And you're seven years old!' said Christabel.

'More like seven months!' said Godfrey.

'Baby! Baby!' said Josie.

Great-Grandmother was to come that year for Christmas; none of the children had seen her before because she had been living in Canada. 'Where's Canada?' asked Elizabeth.

'Be quiet,' said Christabel.

Great-Grandmother was Mother's mother's mother. 'And very old,' said Mother.

'How old?' asked Elizabeth.

'Ssh,' said Godfrey.

There was to be a surprise, the children were to march into the drawing room and sing a carol, and when the carol was ended Great-Grandmother was to be given a basket of roses. But the basket was not a plain basket; it was made, Mother told them, of crystal.

'What's crystal?' asked Elizabeth.

'Shut up,' said Josie, but, 'It's the very finest glass,' said Mother.

The roses were not plain roses either; they were Christmas roses, snow-white. Elizabeth had expected them to be scarlet. *'Isn't* she silly?' said Josie.

Who was to carry the basket? Who was to give it? 'I'm the eldest,' said Christabel. 'It ought to be me.'

'I'm the boy,' said Godfrey. 'It ought to be me.'

'I'm Josephine after Great-Grandmother,' said Josie. 'It ought to be me.'

'Who is to give it? Who?' In the end they asked Mother, and Mother said 'Elizabeth.'

'Elizabeth?'

'Elizabeth?'

'Elizabeth?'

'Why?' They all wanted to know.

'Because she's the youngest,' said Mother.

None of them had heard that as a reason before, and –

'It's too heavy for her,' said Christabel.

'She'll drop it,' said Godfrey.

'You know what she is,' said Josie.

'I'll be very, very careful,' said Elizabeth.

How proud she was when Mother gave the handsome, shining basket into her hands outside the drawing-room door! It was so heavy that her arms ached, but she would not have given it up for anything in the world. Her heart beat under her velvet dress, her cheeks were red, as they marched in and stood in a row before Great-Grandmother. 'Noel, Noel,' they sang.

Great-Grandmother was sitting in the armchair; she had a white shawl over her knees and a white scarf patterned with silver over her shoulders; to Elizabeth she looked as if she were dressed in white and silver all over; she even had white hair, and in one hand she held a thin stick with a silver top. She had something else, and Elizabeth stopped in the middle of a note; at the end of Great-Grandmother's nose hung a dewdrop.

*

An older, cleverer child might have thought, Why doesn't Great-Grandmother blow her nose? But to Elizabeth that trembling, shining drop was beautiful; it caught the shine from the Christmas tree and, if Great-Grandmother moved, it twinkled; it reminded Elizabeth of something, she could not think what – can you? – and she gazed at it. She gazed so hard that she did not hear the carol end.

'. . . Born is the King of Is-ra-el.'

There was silence.

'Eliza*beth*!' hissed Christabel.

'Go *on*,' whispered Godfrey.

Josie gave Elizabeth a push.

Elizabeth jumped and dropped the basket.

The Christmas roses were scattered on the carpet, and the crystal basket was broken to bits.

Hours afterward – it was really one hour, but to Elizabeth it felt like hours – Mother came upstairs. 'Great-Grandmother wants to see you,' she said.

Elizabeth was down behind the chest. The velvet dress was dusty now, but she did not care. She had not come out to have tea nor to see her presents. 'What's the use of giving Elizabeth presents?' she heard Father say. 'She doesn't ride the one she has.'

Elizabeth had made herself flatter and flatter behind the cedar chest; now she raised her head. 'Great-Grandmother *wants* to see me?' she asked.

Great-Grandmother looked at Elizabeth, at her face, which was red and swollen with tears, at her hands that had dropped the basket, at her legs that were too short to ride the bicycle, at her dusty dress.

'H'm,' said a voice. 'Something will have to be done.'

It must have been Great-Grandmother's voice; there was nobody else in the room; but it seemed to come from high up, a long way up, from the top of the tree, for instance; at the same moment there was a swishing sound as of something brushing through branches, wings perhaps, and the fairy doll came flying – it was falling, of course, but it sounded like flying – down from the tree to the carpet. She landed by Great-Grandmother's stick.

'Dear me! How fortunate,' said Great-Grandmother, and now her voice certainly came from her. 'I was just going to say you needed a good fairy.'

'Me?' asked Elizabeth.

'You,' said Great-Grandmother. 'You had better have this one.'

Elizabeth looked at the fairy doll, and the fairy doll looked at Elizabeth; the wand was still stirring with the rush of the fall.

'What about the others?' asked Elizabeth.

'You can leave the others to me,' said Great Grandmother.

'What about next Christmas and the tree?'

'Next Christmas is a long way off,' said Great-Grandmother. 'We'll wait and see.'

Slowly Elizabeth knelt down on the floor and picked up the fairy doll.

Chapter 2

'How can I take care of her?' asked Elizabeth.

'She is to take care of you,' said Mother, but as you know if you have read any fairy stories, fairies have a way of doing things the wrong way round.

'Pooh! She's only an ordinary doll dressed up in fairy clothes,' said Josie, who was jealous.

'She's not ordinary,' said Elizabeth, and, as you will see, Elizabeth was right.

'What's her name?' asked Josie.

'She doesn't need a name. She's Fairy Doll,' said Elizabeth, and, 'How dare I take care of her?' she asked.

Fairy Doll looked straight in front of her, but Elizabeth must have touched the wand; it stirred gently, very gently, in Fairy Doll's hand.

'Where will she live?' asked Josie. 'She can't live in the dolls' house. Fairies don't live anywhere,' said Josie scornfully.

'They must,' said Elizabeth. 'Mother says some people think fairies were the first people, so they must have lived somewhere.' And she went and asked Father, 'Father, where did the first people live?'

'In caves, I expect,' said Father.

'Elizabeth can't make a cave,' said Josie.

Elizabeth had just opened her mouth to say, 'No,' when 'Ting' went a sound in her head. It was as clear and small as one of the glass Christmas bells.

'Ting. Bicycle basket,' it said.

Elizabeth knew what a cave was like; there had been caves at the seaside; there was one in the big wood across the field, and this very Christmas there was a clay model cave, in the Crèche, at school. If she had been a clever child she would have argued, 'Bicycle basket? Not a *bicycle* basket?' but, not being clever, she went to look. She unstrapped the basket from her bicycle and put it on its side.

The 'ting' had been right; the bicycle basket, on its side, was exactly the shape of a cave.

The cave in the wood had grass on its top, brambles and bracken and trees and grass. 'What's fairy grass?' asked Elizabeth, and 'Ting,' a word rang in her head. The word was 'moss'.

She knew where moss was; they had gathered some from the wood for the Christmas-tree tub. A week ago Elizabeth would not have gone to the wood alone, but now she had Fairy Doll and she set out through the garden, across the road and fields; soon she was back with her skirt held up full of moss.

She covered the outside of the bicycle basket with the moss like a cosy green thatch; then she stood the basket on a box and made a moss lawn around it. 'Later on I'll have beds of tiny real flowers,' she said.

It is odd how quickly you get used to things; Elizabeth asked, and the 'ting' answered; it was a little like a slot machine. 'What shall I put on the floor?' she asked.

'Ting. In the garage.'

A cleverer child would have said, 'In the *garage*?' Josie, for instance, would not have gone there at all, but Elizabeth went, and there, in the garage, Father was sawing up logs.

'What did they put on the cave floors?' asked Elizabeth.

'Sand, I expect,' said Father.

Sand was far, far away, at the seaside; Elizabeth was just going to say, with a sigh, that that was no good when she looked at the pile of sawdust that had fallen from the logs, and, 'Sawdust! Fairy sand,' said the 'ting'.

'What about a bed?' said Josie.

'A bed?' asked Elizabeth, and back came the 'ting'. 'Try a shell.'

'A coconut shell?' asked Elizabeth, watching the

blue tits swinging on the bird table, but a coconut seemed coarse and rough for a little fairy doll. A shell? A shell? Why not a real shell? Elizabeth had brought one back from the seaside; she had not picked it up, the landlady had given it to her; it was big, deep pink inside, and if you held it to your ear you heard, far off, the sound of the sea; it sounded like a lullaby. Fairy Doll could lie in the shell and listen; it made a little private radio.

The shell needed a mattress. 'Flowers,' said the 'ting'.

Josie would have answered that there were no flowers now, but, 'Is there a soft winter flower, like feathers?' asked Elizabeth. 'Ting' came the answer. 'Old man's beard.'

Do you know old man's beard that hangs on the trees and the hedges from autumn to winter? Its seeds hang in a soft fluff, and Elizabeth picked a handful of it; then she found a deep red leaf for a cover; it was from the Virginia creeper that grew up the front of the house.

Soon the cave was finished – 'and with fairy things,' said Elizabeth. She asked Father to cut her two bits from a round, smooth branch; they were three inches high and made a table and a writing

desk. There were toadstools for stools; stuck in the sawdust, they stood upright. On the table were acorn cups and bowls, and small leaf plates. Over the writing desk was a piece of dried-out honey-comb; it was exactly like the rack of pigeonholes over Father's desk. Fairy Doll could keep her letters there, and she could write letters; Elizabeth found a tiny feather and asked Godfrey to cut its point to make a quill pen like the one Mother had, and for writing paper there were petals of a Christmas rose. If you scratch a petal with a pen, or, better still, a pin, it makes fairy marks. 'Later on there'll be all sorts of flower writing-paper,' said Elizabeth.

There was a broom made of a fir-twig, a burr for

a doorscraper; a berry on a thread made a knocker. 'In summer I'll get you a dandelion clock,' she told Fairy Doll.

'You haven't got a bath,' said Josie.

'Fairies don't need baths,' said Elizabeth. 'They wash outside in the dew.'

It was odd; she was beginning to know about fairies.

'What does she eat?' asked Josie.

'Snow ice-cream,' said Elizabeth – it was snowing – 'holly baked apples, and hips off the rose trees.'

'Hips are too big for a little doll like that,' said Josie.

'They are fairy pineapples,' said Elizabeth with dignity.

'Look what Elizabeth has made,' cried Christabel, and she said in surprise, 'It's pretty!'

Godfrey came to look. 'Gosh!' said Godfrey.

Josie put her hand to touch a toadstool, and a funny feeling stirred inside Elizabeth, a feeling like a hard little wand.

'Don't touch,' said Elizabeth to Josie.

*

Spring came, and Fairy Doll had a hat made out of crocus, and a pussywillow-fuzz powder puff; she ate fairy bananas, which were bunches of catkins – rather than large bananas – and fairy lettuces, which were hawthorn buds – rather small; she ate French rolls, the gold-brown beech-leaf buds, with primrose butter; the beds in the moss lawn were planted with violets out of the wood.

One morning, as they were all starting off to school, Christabel said, as usual, 'Elizabeth, you haven't brushed your teeth.'

Elizabeth was going back when she stopped. 'But I have,' she said. She had been in the bathroom, and 'Ting. Brush your teeth' had come in her head. 'I've brushed them,' said Elizabeth, amazed. Christabel was amazed as well.

A few days afterward Miss Thrupp said in school, 'Let's see what Elizabeth can do,' which meant, 'Let's see what Elizabeth can't do.' 'Stand up, Elizabeth, and say the seven-times table.'

'Seven times one are seven,' said Elizabeth, and there was a long, long pause.

'Seven times two?' Miss Thrupp said encouragingly.

Elizabeth stood dumb, and the class began to laugh.

'Hush, children. Seven times two . . .'

'Ting. Are fourteen.' And Elizabeth went on. 'Seven threes are twenty-one, seven fours are twenty-eight . . .' right up to 'Seven twelves are eighty-four.'

At the end Miss Thrupp and the children were staring. Then they clapped.

In reading they had come to 'The Sto-ry of the Sleep-ing Beau-ty.' Elizabeth looked hopelessly at all the difficult words; her eyes were just beginning to fill with tears when, 'Ting,' the words 'Lilac Fairy' seemed to skip off the page into her head. 'It says "Lilac Fairy,"' she said.

'Go on,' said Miss Thrupp, 'go on,' and Elizabeth went on. 'Li-lac Fai-ry. Spin-ning Wheel. Prince Charm-ing.' 'Ting. Ting. Ting,' went the bell.

'Good girl, those are difficult words!' said Miss Thrupp.

In sewing they began tray-cloths in embroidery stitches; perhaps it was from making the small-sized fairy things that Elizabeth's fingers had learned to be neat; the needle went in and out, plock, plock, plock, and there was not a trace of blood. 'You're getting quite nimble,' said Miss Thrupp, and she told the class, 'Nimble means clever and quick.'

'Does she mean I'm *clever*?' Elizabeth asked the little boy next to her. She could not believe it.

Soon it was summer. Fairy Doll had a Canterbury bell for a hat; her bed had a peony-petal cover now. She ate daisy poached eggs, rose-petal ham, and lavender rissoles. Lady's slipper and pimpernels were planted in the moss.

'What's the matter with Elizabeth?' asked Godfrey. 'She not half such a little duffer as she was.'

That was true. She was allowed to take the Sunday newspapers in for Father, and Mother trusted her to wash up by herself.

'You can use my paint box if you like,' said Christabel.

'You can take your own bus money,' said Josie.

'Run to the shop,' said Mother, 'and get me a mop and a packet of matches, a pot of strawberry jam, half a pound of butter, and a pound of ginger nuts.'

'What have you brought?' she asked when Elizabeth came back.

'A pound of ginger nuts, half a pound of butter, a pot of strawberry jam, a packet of matches, and a mop,' said Elizabeth, counting them out.

'But you still can't ride the bicycle,' said Josie.

It grew hot. Fairy Doll had a nasturtium leaf for a sunshade, and Elizabeth made her a poppy doll. To make a poppy doll you turn the petals back and tie them down with a grass blade for a sash; the middle of the poppy makes the head, with the fuzz for hair, and for arms you take a bit of poppy stalk and thread it through under the petals; then the poppy doll is complete, except that it has only one leg. Perhaps that was why Fairy Doll did not play with hers.

Something was the matter with Fairy Doll; her dress had become a little draggled and dirty after all these months, but it was more than that; her wings looked limp, the wand in her hand was still.

Something was the matter in Elizabeth too; the bell did not say, 'Ting' any more in her head. 'Dull, dull, dull,' it said.

'Dull?' asked Elizabeth.

'Dull. Dull. Dull.' It was more like a drum than a bell.

'Does it mean Fairy Doll is dull with me?' asked Elizabeth.

She felt sad; then she felt ashamed.

A fairy likes flying. Naturally. If you had wings

you would like fly-
ing too. Sometimes
Elizabeth would
hold Fairy Doll
up in the air and
run with
her; then
the wings
would lift,
the wand would
wave, the gauze
dress fly back, but
Elizabeth was too
plump to run for long.

'I'll put her on my bicycle and fly her,' Godfrey
offered.

'You mustn't touch her,' cried Elizabeth.

'Well, fly her yourself,' said Godfrey, offended,
and he rode off.

'Fly her yourself.' 'Ting' went the bell, and it was
a bell, not a drum. 'Ting. Ting. Fly. Fly.' So that was
what Fairy Doll was wishing! Elizabeth went
slowly into the garage and looked at the pale blue,
still brand-new bicycle.

*

'It doesn't hurt so much to fall off in summer as in winter,' said Elizabeth, but her voice trembled. Her fingers trembled too, as she tied Fairy Doll onto the handlebars.

Then Elizabeth put her foot on the pedal. 'Push. Pedal, pedal,' she said and shut her eyes, but you cannot ride even the smallest bicycle with your eyes shut.

She had to open them, but it was too late to stop. The drive from the garage led down a slope to the gate, and 'Ting,' away went the bicycle with Elizabeth on it. For a moment she wobbled; then she saw the silver wings filling and thrilling as they rushed through the air, and the wand blew round and round. 'Pedal. Pedal, pedal.' It might have been Christabel talking, but it was not. 'Pedal.' Elizabeth's hair was blown back, the wind rushed past her; she felt she was flying too; she came to the gate and fell off. 'Ow!' groaned Elizabeth, but she had flown. She knew what Fairy Doll wanted. Her leg was bleeding, but she turned the bicycle round to start off down the drive again.

Elizabeth was late for tea.

'What *have* you been doing?' asked Christabel. 'There's no jam left.' But Elizabeth did not care.

'You've torn your frock. All the buns are gone,' said Godfrey, but Elizabeth did not care.

'You're all over scratches and dust,' said Josie. 'We've eaten the cake.' But Elizabeth still did not care.

'Well, where have you been?' asked Mother.

Elizabeth answered, 'Riding my bicycle.'

*

Christabel was pleased. Godfrey was very pleased, but Josie said, 'Pooh! It isn't Elizabeth who does things, it's Fairy Doll.'

'Is it?' asked Elizabeth.

'Try without her and you'll see,' said Josie.

Elizabeth looked at Fairy Doll, who was sitting by her on the table. 'But I'm not without her,' said Elizabeth.

Autumn came and brought the fruit; briony berries were fairy plums and greengages; a single black-berry pip was a grape. A hazel nut was pork with crackling. In every garden people were making bonfires, and Elizabeth made one in the fairy gar-den; it was of pine needles and twigs, and she watched it carefully; its smoke went up no bigger than a feather. It was altogether a fairy time. In the wood she found toadstools so close together that they looked like chairs put ready for a concert; she gave a fairy concert, but, 'It ought to be crickets and nightingales,' said Elizabeth. There were silver trails over the leaves and grass. 'Fairy paths,' she said.

'Snails,' snapped Josie. No doubt about it, Josie was jealous.

School began, and Elizabeth was moved up; she was learning the twelve-times table, reading to herself, and knitting a scarf. She was allowed to ride her bicycle on the main road, and to stay up till half-past seven every night.

Then, on a late October day when the first frost was on the grass, Fairy Doll was lost.

Chapter 3

'You must have dropped her on the road,' said Mother.

'But I didn't.'

'Perhaps you left her at school.'

'I didn't.'

'In your satchel.' 'In your pocket . . .' 'On the counter in the shop.' 'In the bathroom.' 'On the bookshelf.' 'Behind the clock.' 'Up in the apple tree.'

'I didn't. I didn't. I didn't,' sobbed Elizabeth.

Everyone was very kind. They all looked everywhere, high and low, up and down, in and out. Godfrey said he looked under every leaf in the whole garden that was big enough. It was no good. Fairy Doll was lost.

Elizabeth went and lay down on the floor behind

the cedar chest; she only came out to have a cup of milk and go to bed.

Next morning she went behind the chest and lay down again.

'Make her come out,' said Josie, who seemed curiously worried.

'Leave her alone,' said Mother.

'She must come out. She has to go to school.' But Elizabeth would not go to school. How could she? She could not say her tables now, or spell or read or sew, and she had not brushed her teeth. The tears made a wet place in the dust on the floor. 'And I can't ride my bicycle,' she said.

It was Christabel's birthday. Christabel was twelve. Elizabeth had a present done up in yellow paper; it was a peppermint lollipop, but she did not give it to Christabel.

She stayed most of the day behind the cedar chest, and a day can feel like weeks when you are seven years old.

'Make her come out,' said Josie.

At four o'clock Mother came up. 'Great-Grandmother has come for the birthday tea,' she said.

'Great-Grandmother?' Elizabeth lay very still.

'I should come down if I were you,' said Mother.

Last time Great-Grandmother came she had sent for Elizabeth and Elizabeth had come with a tearstained face. It was tearstained now, but, 'I could wash it,' said Elizabeth and from somewhere she thought she heard a 'ting'. Her dress had been dirty; it was dirty now, but, 'I could change it,' said Elizabeth, and she heard another 'ting'. It was faint and faraway; it could not have been a 'ting' because the chest was empty, the fairy doll was gone, but it sounded like a 'ting'. Very slowly Elizabeth sat up.

'Good afternoon, Elizabeth,' said Great-Grandmother. No one else took any notice as Elizabeth, brushed and clean, in a clean dress, put the present by Christabel and slid into her own place.

She was stiff from lying on the floor, her head ached and her throat was sore from crying, and she was hungry.

Mother gave her a cup of tea; the tea was sweet and hot, and there were minced chicken sandwiches with lettuce, shortcake biscuits, chocolate tarts, sponge fingers, and meringues, besides the birthday cake. Mother passed the sandwiches to Elizabeth and gave her another cup of tea. Elizabeth began to feel much better.

Christabel's cake was pink and white. It had CHRISTABEL, HAPPY BIRTHDAY written on it, and twelve candles.

'And I,' said Great-Grandmother, 'am eight times twelve.' A dewdrop slid down her nose and twinkled. 'Eight times twelve. Who can tell me what that is?' asked Great-Grandmother.

With her eyes on the dewdrop, before any of the others could answer – 'Ting.' 'Ninety-six,' said Elizabeth.

After tea they had races. One was The Button, the Thread, and the Needle. 'I can race that,' said Great-Grandmother. 'I'll have Elizabeth for my partner.'

Great-Grandmother threaded the needle as she sat in a chair. Elizabeth had to run with the button, sew it to a patch of cloth, and run back. 'I can't . . .' she began, but, 'Nimble fingers,' said Great-Grandmother; the stitches flew in and out, the button was on, Elizabeth ran back, and she and Great-Grandmother won the double prize, magic pencils that wrote in four colours.

'Dear me, how annoying!' said Great-Grandmother. 'I had meant to stop at the shop and get a few things – some silver polish, a packet of

Lux, a one-and-sixpenny duster, and a nutmeg – and I forgot. Elizabeth, hop on your bicycle and get them for me.'

'But I can't . . .'

'Here's five shillings,' said Great-Grandmother. 'Bring me the change.'

'Ting.' Before Elizabeth knew where she was, she was out on the road, riding her bicycle and perfectly steady. Soon she was back with all the things and one-and-fourpence change for Great-Grandmother.

'Then were the "tings" me?' asked Elizabeth, puzzled. She could not believe it. 'I thought they were Fairy Doll.'

'I thought so too,' said Josie. She sounded disappointed.

'How could they be?' asked Godfrey.

'They couldn't,' said Christabel, who after all was twelve now and ought to know. 'Don't be silly,' said Christabel. 'She was just a doll.'

'*Fairy* Doll.' It was Great-Grandmother who corrected Christabel, but her voice sounded high up and far away – As if it came from somewhere else? asked Elizabeth.

Chapter 4

In the country, November and December are the best times for hedges, but now no one picked the old man's beard for a mattress, or winter berries to bake; no one went to the wood for fresh moss and new toadstools. The fairy house was broken up; the bicycle basket was on the bicycle.

For Christmas they each chose what they would get.

'A writing case,' said Christabel.

'A reversing engine, Number Fifty-one, for my Hornby trains,' said Godfrey.

'A kitchen set,' said Josie.

Elizabeth did not know what she wanted. 'Another fairy doll?' suggested Christabel.

'Another! There isn't another,' said Elizabeth, shocked. 'She was Fairy Doll.'

On Christmas Eve the tree was set up in the drawing room. Mother opened the cedar chest and brought the decorations down, the tinsel and the icicles, the witch balls and trumpets and bells, the lights and candle clips. There were new candles, new boxes of sweets, new little bags of nuts, shining new coins, and new crackers. 'But what shall we put at the top?' asked Christabel.

Elizabeth ran out of the room, upstairs to the cedar chest.

She was going to cast herself down – 'and stay there; I don't want Christmas,' said Elizabeth – but the lid of the chest was open, and, on top of a pile of blankets and folded summer vests, she saw the cotton-reel box that had held Fairy Doll.

'Empty,' said Elizabeth. 'Empty.'

She was just beginning to sob when, 'Look in the box,' went a loud, clear 'ting'. 'Look in the box.'

Elizabeth stopped in the middle of a sob, but she was cleverer now, and she argued. 'Why?' asked Elizabeth.

The 'ting' took no notice. 'Look in the box.'

'Why? It's *empty*.'

'Look in the box.'

'It's *empty*.'

'Look.'

It was more than a 'ting', it was a stir, as if the box were alive, as if – a wand were waving?

Slowly Elizabeth put out her hand. The lid of the box flew off – 'Did I open it?' asked Elizabeth. She heard the blue tissue paper rustle – 'Did I rustle it?' – and out, in her hand, came Fairy Doll.

'But how?' asked Christabel. 'How? And how did Elizabeth *know*? I said, "What shall we put on top?" and –'

'She ran straight upstairs,' said Godfrey, 'and came back with Fairy Doll –'

'Who was lost,' said Josie. 'Wasn't she lost?'

'We don't understand,' they said, all three together.

*

You may think that when Josie was jealous she stole Fairy Doll and put her back in the cedar chest. I thought so too, but then why was Josie so surprised? And how was it that Fairy Doll was not draggled at all, but clean, in a fresh new dress, with new silver wings and another pair of mice-sewn shoes?

Perhaps it was Mother who found her and put her away because it was time that Elizabeth had 'tings' of her own. Mother could have made the dress and wings, but, 'I couldn't have sewn those shoes,' said Mother.

Fairy Doll looked straight in front of her, and the wand stirred gently, very gently in her hand.

Chapter 5

Fairy Doll went back in her place on the top of the Christmas tree. After Christmas she was laid away in the cedar chest till next year. 'She has done her work,' said Mother.

Christabel had her writing case; Godfrey had his engine; Josie, who was cured of being jealous, had a kitchen set with pots and pans, a pastry board, a rolling pin, and a kettle. Elizabeth had a long-clothes baby doll, with eyes that opened and shut.

She loves the baby doll, but every time she goes up and down the stairs she stops on the landing and puts her hand on the cedar chest; every time she does it – it may be her imagination – from

inside comes a faint glass 'ting' that is like a
Christmas bell.

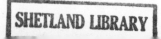

RUMER GODDEN

The Story of Holly & Ivy

It is the day before Christmas and the toys in Mr Blossom's shop know it is their last chance to be sold. Holly, a small doll dressed especially for Christmas, wishes hardest of all for her own special child. But the day ends and Holly is left in the window.

Early on Christmas morning, a little lost girl finds herself outside the toyshop. Ivy has never had a doll to love. Or a family to love her. When she sees Holly, she knows at once that this doll is meant especially for her. And Holly knows that this girl is the one she was wishing for. But Ivy has no money, and the shop is closed. There will be no Christmas Day for Holly and Ivy – will there?

RUMER GODDEN

The
Dolls' House

Tottie is a little, pretty wooden doll with glossy black hair, painted pink cheeks and bright blue eyes that are very determined. She and her doll family are owned by two sisters, Emily and Charlotte, and are very happy. Except for one thing: they long to move out of their shoebox and into a proper home. So they wish, and they wish, and they wish. All their dreams come true when Emily and Charlotte fix up an old dolls' house, just for them.

Then Marchpane arrives. She is a valuable and elegant doll with long blonde hair and a beautiful wedding dress. But Marchpane is also vain and very cruel – and she wants to take over the dolls' house. Suddenly Tottie's family is in terrible danger. Now they must wish, and wish, and wish . . .

A selected list of titles available from Macmillan Children's Books

RUMER GODDEN

Miss Happiness and Miss Flower	ISBN-13: 978-1-4050-8856-5	£10.99
	ISBN-10: 1-4050-8856-7	
The Story of Holly and Ivy	ISBN-13: 978-0-330-43974-9	£4.99
	ISBN-10: 0-330-43974-X	
The Dolls' House	ISBN-13: 978-0-330-44255-8	£4.99
	ISBN-10: 0-330-44255-4	

For older readers

The Peacock Spring	ISBN-13: 978-0-330-39738-4	£5.99
	ISBN-10: 0-330-39738-9	
The Greengage Summer	ISBN-13: 978-0-330-39737-7	£5.99
	ISBN-10: 0-330-39737-0	